The Family Christmas Treasury

TALES of ANTICIPATION, CELEBRATION, and JOY

Houghton Mifflin Harcourt

Boston New York

Christmas is a special time of year for story sharing . . .

'Tis the season for sipping cocoa, trimming the tree, and revisiting your favorite Christmas stories. *The Family Christmas Treasury* is a collection of timeless holiday tales sure to put you in the spirit of the season. Catch up with your favorite characters at Christmastime, including Curious George, Strega Nona, Lyle the Crocodile, Tacky the Penguin, and many more! Whether nestled 'round the fire or snuggled up in bed, get cozy with your little one and open the pages of this treasury to experience the most wonderful time of the year.

Contents

MARGRET AND H. A. REY'S

Merry Christmas, Curious George

Written by Cathy Hapka

Illustrated in the style of H. A. Rey by Mary O'Keefe Young

This is George.
He lived with his friend, the man with the yellow hat.
He was a good little monkey and always very curious.

Today George was visiting a Christmas tree farm.

"You can help me pick out the perfect tree for our home," his friend told him. "Keep close to me while we look."

George promised to be good, but little monkeys sometimes forget . . .

The Christmas tree farm had more trees than George had ever seen.

He found a very nice one right away . . .

But then another caught his eye . . .

. . . and then one more . . . and then another.

George was curious. How many Christmas trees could there be?

George could not resist climbing up the tallest tree to get a better view.

He looked for the man with the yellow hat. But his friend was nowhere in sight.

Two men tromped into the clearing.

"There's our tree!" one man told the other.

The men cut down the tree and loaded it onto a truck—

—along with George! George held on tightly. He saw the man with the yellow hat as the truck drove away, but the truck was going too fast. George could not jump off. He was scared, but still a little curious.

Soon the truck stopped in front of a hospital.
George peeked out of the branches as the men carried his tree inside.

The hospital was a busy place.
George jumped out of the tree.

There was lots here to see and do!
He looked at some interesting pictures.

He found a jacket and tried it on.

He played on a trampoline.

He even went for a ride on a speedy little cart. What fun!

Then George spotted something *very* interesting. His tree!

George knew that Christmas trees were supposed to have tinsel and twinkling lights and shiny ornaments. But this tree was empty.

George thought and thought—and then he had an idea.

Next George noticed a pile of gifts in the corner of the room.

The gifts looked pretty. But George was curious. Could he make them look even prettier?

This red bow would look much better on the green box. And the nametags might look nicer on different packages, too . . .

A nurse arrived, and what did she see? "A monkey! And he's making a big mess!"

A group of children crowded around the nurse. They were all patients at the hospital. Even though it was almost Christmas, the children were not smiling or looking happy.

"Come along," the nurse said, picking George up. "I'd better get you out of here before you can ruin anything else."

A girl with a cast stared at George's tree. Suddenly she giggled. "Look," she said.
"It's my x-ray!"

A boy laughed. "And there's the balloon from my room."

All the children started chattering and laughing as they looked at George's funny
decorations.

"Can't he stay for the party?" a boy asked the nurse. "We don't mind about the gifts. It will be fun to sort them out."

"Please let him stay! Please!" the other children chimed in.

When she saw how happy the children looked, the nurse looked happier, too. "I suppose he can stay," she said. "IF he promises to help fix the tree!"

George was happy to help. The children helped, too. Some of them returned George's decorations, while others handed George the real ornaments. He scampered up and down, stringing lights and hanging tinsel. Being a monkey, he was good at that sort of thing.

He was also good at making the children laugh.

When the tree was finished, George helped open the gifts. He was having such a good time that he completely forgot he was lost . . .

. . . until the man with the yellow hat hurried into the room. "There you are, George!" he cried. "I followed that truck all the way here."

George was very happy to be reunited with his friend. The nurse invited them both to stay for milk and cookies.

"Ho ho ho! Did someone mention milk and cookies?"
A man in a red suit walked into the room, his belly
jiggling. He was holding a beautiful golden star.

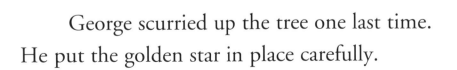

George's eyes widened. It was Santa Claus!
"Who would like to put the star on top of
the tree?" Santa asked.
"George!" the children cried at once. "Let
George do it!"

George scurried up the tree one last time.
He put the golden star in place carefully.

MERRY CHRISTMAS, CURIOUS GEORGE!

29

CHRISTMAS TREE

O CHRISTMAS TREE, O Christmas tree,
how lovely are your branches.
In summer sun, in winter snow,
a dress of green you always show.
O Christmas tree, O Christmas tree,
how lovely are your branches.

O Christmas tree, O Christmas tree,
with happiness we greet you.
When decked with candles once a year,
you fill our hearts with Yuletide cheer.
O Christmas tree, O Christmas tree,
with happiness we greet you.

Tacky's Christmas

Written by Helen Lester
Illustrated by Lynn Munsinger

To the best Christmas gifts I've ever had:
Robin, Rob & Jodi, Jamie & Danyle, Kate, Andrew
—and those to come.
Thanks, H

For Penny's grandsons, Lionel and Tiernan.
—L

Christmas had come to Nice Icy Land.

Excitement was in the air.

And in the water.

And in the ice cubes.

Goodly, Lovely, Angel, Neatly, and Perfect had everything beautifully organized.

"First we must wrap our presents," they said.

But wait. Where was Tacky?

Where Tacky *was* was in the chimney.

Practicing.

And stuck.

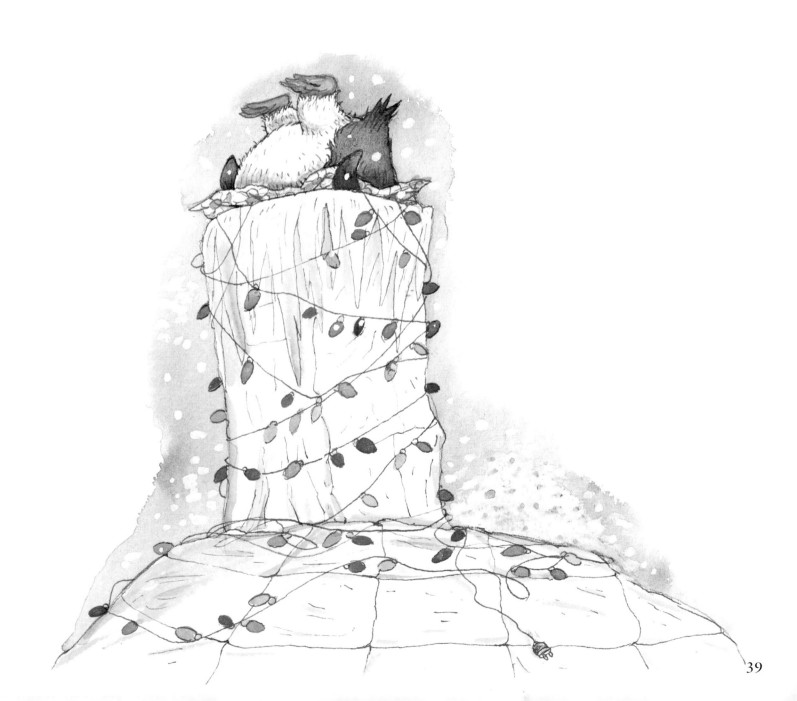

He had been selected to wear the Santa outfit since his belly
shook like a bowl full of jelly when he laughed.

Eventually his companions found him, and
with much huffing and oofing

—*phwwop*—

they pulled him out.

41

Present wrapping was very secret, so each penguin hid behind
a block of ice.

Shh . . .

Now that the presents were wrapped, it was time to turn to the
task of making ornaments. As they worked with glue and glitter
and sequins, the penguins sang their favorite carol:

Deck the iceberg, wrap a gifty
Fa la la la la la la la la
Make an ornament that's nifty
Fa la la la la la la la la
Hang it on a tree—

A tree?
The penguins looked around.

There seemed to be a shortage of trees
in Nice Icy Land.

"We could decorate Tacky," suggested Goodly and Lovely.

"He's sort of tree-shaped, if a bit heavy on the lower part,"
added Angel, Neatly, and Perfect.
"Hey, suit me up!" cried Tacky.

And so they did.

49

It was a red tree and they'd been dreaming of
a green Christmas, but never mind.

With the presents under the Tackytree,
there was only one thing left to do.

Open the gifts!

Goodly gave each penguin a jar of
belly-sliding slickum.

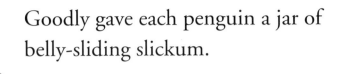

Lovely offered zippy speed flippers.

Angel's gift was snappy bow ties.

Neatly provided feather dusters
so they could dust their feathers.

Perfect gave bottles of Yellow
Brand Beak and Foot Polish.

Finally, Tacky presented each of his companions with

A CAN OF SHAVING CREAM.

Shaving cream? For penguins?
Goodly, Lovely, Angel, Neatly, and Perfect were speechless.
So Tacky took over.
"Hey, this is really fun stuff. Let me show you."
And then squirt . . .
Goodly, Lovely, Angel, Neatly, and Perfect were about to duck
when suddenly they were interrupted by the *thump* . . .
thump . . . *thump* of feet in the distance.

"Oh, no!" they cried. "It's the hunters. On Christmas yet!"

But Tacky was in full squirt mode.

He zapped Goodly and Lovely, who pleaded, "Tacky, the hunters are coming!"

"This is so cool!" *Squirt.* Angel got it next.

And meanwhile, the hunters were approaching with rocks and locks and maps and traps, and they were rough and tough.

As the *thump . . . thump . . . thump* drew closer, the penguins could hear their growly voices chanting,

We're gonna march some pretty penguins
And we'll drag 'em through the snow
And we'll take away their Christmas giftzies
HO. HO. HO.

"Puh-lease, Tacky!" begged his companions.
But Tacky was having too much fun.
He squirted Neatly and Perfect.
"Here ya go!"
It takes a lot to make a penguin shiver, but by now
Goodly, Lovely, Angel, Neatly, and Perfect were
crouching behind Tacky. Shivering.
The hunters drew closer and closer, and finally they
thumped right up to Tacky.

Stopped.

Then stared.

And then, most surprising, they broke into big silly grins.

"Whoa! Him's not a pretty penguin. Him's
Sandy Clawz! Looky that beardy! And him's
got jewels and sequins and sprinkles.
Gotta be Sandy Clawz!"

Shyly, respectfully, adoringly, the hunters bowed.

Goodly, Lovely, Angel, Neatly, and Perfect peeked out
from behind Tacky. The hunters gasped.

"Why, looky, them's Sandy's elfies! Them's got
beardzes too. Whoa, looky that!
Merry Christmas, elfies!"

"Merry Christmas," the penguins
bubbled back.

Well, of course, there was only one thing to do.
After all, it was Christmas. A special time of giving and sharing.
So the penguins invited the hunters to stay and enjoy
their fish pudding.
Tacky came down the chimney.
Before dinner.

They sang and played games and told jokes, and everyone was filled with the Christmas spirit and had the merriest Christmas ever.

And much, much later, after the happy hunters had departed, Goodly, Lovely, Angel, Neatly, and Perfect hugged Tacky. Tacky was an odd bird, but a nice bird to have around —especially at Christmas.

COME, ALL YE FAITHFUL

O COME ALL YE FAITHFUL, joyful and triumphant,
O come ye, O come ye to Bethlehem.
Come and behold Him, born the King of angels.

O come let us adore Him,
O come let us adore Him,
O come let us adore Him,
Christ the Lord.

Sing, choirs of angels, sing in exultation,
Sing all ye citizens of heav'n above.
Glory to God, glory in the highest.

For Grampa Martin

The Finest Christmas Tree

John and Ann Hassett

Farmer Tuttle was a Christmas tree farmer.
His forest was full of pointy-topped trees.
Children liked to hear the chop of his ax and
the cheery putt-putt of his tractor.

Every Christmas
Farmer Tuttle
piled the trees onto his
truck for a trip to the city.
He sold his trees from a
busy street corner. He
helped shoppers pick a
tree that was just right—
not too big and not too
small.

When all his trees were sold, he shopped
at the city stores for a special gift.
Farmer Tuttle always bought Mrs. Tuttle
a new Christmas hat.

But one Christmas, shoppers did not stop to buy
Farmer Tuttle's trees.
"Smart shoppers want trees made of plastic," said a man.
"Plastic trees are positively perfect," a lady said.
"Plastic trees go back in the attic till next Christmas,"
said another.
Farmer Tuttle piled his trees back onto the truck.
There was no money to buy Mrs. Tuttle a
new Christmas hat.

Farmer Tuttle
did not go
into the forest
anymore.

The next winter, a man from the sawmill
offered to buy all the trees in the
forest. He wanted to saw the trees into
toothpicks and clothespins. The man
gave the Tuttles until Christmas to decide.

Farmer Tuttle wondered what to do. Then, with only one day till Christmas, a strange letter came in the mail. It read:

Dear Farmer Tuttle,
    The workers at our
    factory wish to have
    the finest tree in the forest
    for their Christmas party.
    A crew of cutters
    will arrive shortly.
    Season's greetings,
        The Boss

Farmer Tuttle hurried home with the happy news.
He waited all that day. He waited long into the night,
but the crew of cutters did not come.
"Perhaps they have chosen a plastic tree," he said
to Mrs. Tuttle. He began to think about toothpicks
and clothespins. Farmer Tuttle tugged on his hat
and coat, and he set off for the forest.

Farmer Tuttle was surprised to find small footprints in the snow. He scratched his puzzled head. Paths of tiny footprints wandered from tree to tree all through the forest.

Soon Farmer Tuttle heard the
chop-chop of an ax.
He saw a tall, pointy-topped tree
fall to the snow.

Tiny figures rushed to the tree. They lifted it to their small shoulders. They trotted quickly over the frosty ground and tossed the tree onto the back of a sleigh.

Little voices cheered
as the sleigh raced
over the snow. It
leaped over the treetops.
Up and up the sleigh
flew through the
silent, glimmering
stars, and then it
was gone.

Farmer Tuttle found a box where the tree
had stood. Inside was a beautiful Christmas hat.
He tucked the box under his arm and
hurried home.

Farmer Tuttle's trees still grow in the forest. Every year at Christmas, the crew of cutters returns for another finest tree. Children have seen the tiny footprints in the snow. And Mrs. Tuttle always gets a new Christmas hat.

95

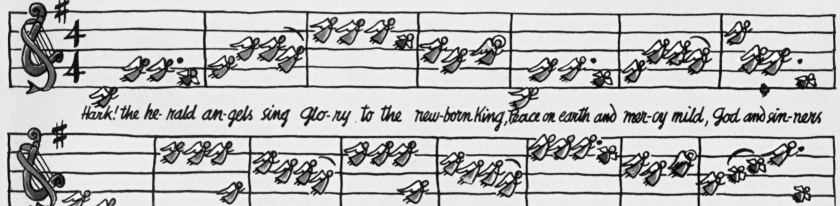

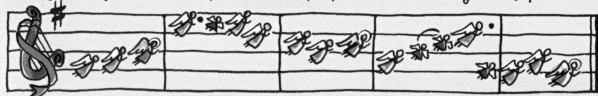

HARK! THE HERALD ANGELS SING

HARK! THE HERALD angels sing,
Glory to the newborn King.
Peace on earth and mercy mild,
God and sinners reconciled.
Joyful all ye nations rise,
Join the triumph of the skies.
With th' angelic host proclaim,
Christ is born in Bethlehem.
Hark! the herald angels sing,
Glory to the newborn King.

Hail the heaven-born Prince of Peace!
Hail the Son of Righteousness!
Light and life to all he brings,
Risen with healing in his wings;
Mild, he lays his glory by,
Born that man no more may die,
Born to raise the sons of earth,
Born to give them second birth:
Hark! the herald angels sing
Glory to the newborn King.

BERNARD WABER

Lyle at Christmas

Christmas was in the air.

It was everywhere.
And everywhere he went,
Lyle the Crocodile was wished
a merry Christmas.
Children gave him big hugs.

So did Millie, the crossing guard.
"That's my special Christmas hug,"
she told him.

Taxi drivers waved cheerily to him,

as did the newsstand owner,
and the pizza man.

Everyone loved Lyle the Crocodile.
And in return Lyle loved the whole wide world.
He loved Bird . . .

and Loretta the cat,
who lived
two houses away
with Mr. Grumps.

He loved East 88th Street, and the house he shared
so happily with Mr. and Mrs. Primm, their children,
Joshua and Miranda, his mother, and Bird.

His only problem
was deciding what gift
he wanted most.

But if Lyle was happy at Christmas, there
was someone living close by who was not at all happy.
That someone was feeling downright miserable, in fact.
And that someone was Mr. Grumps.

"I am having the blahs," moaned Mr. Grumps.
"Those low-down, pit-bottom, yech-ie, yech-ie holiday blahs.
'Tis the season to be jolly. Right? Well, tell me about it."

"Oh, I've tried so hard to get into the spirit of it all,"
Mr. Grumps groaned. "I trimmed the tree.
Wrapped gifts. Hummed a carol or two. Wished for snow.
Roasted chestnuts on an open fire. Did all of that.
And still, I am having the blahs."

Even his adored cat, Loretta, who mostly enjoyed
a sunny disposition, had had it up to her whiskers with
down-in-the-dumps Mr. Grumps and took to moping about.
In her darkest moments, she considered running away.

Everyone tried desperately to cheer Mr. Grumps.
Lyle exhausted his entire repertoire of sure-fire
amusing tricks. Nothing.

Joshua and Miranda baked a huge batch of happy-face
cookies for him, accompanied by a note that read:
Have a nice day. But Mr. Grumps was in no mood
for happy faces. Nor was he about to have a nice day.

Mrs. Primm thought
a game or two of checkers
would divert him, but she soon
discovered that Mr. Grumps
was a mighty sore loser.

Lyle's mother, Nurse Felicity,
checked Mr. Grumps' pulse
and asked him to stick out his tongue.
"No problem with his health,"
she concluded.

Mr. Primm tried telling him
uproarious jokes.
"Heard it," Mr. Grumps said,
cutting him short.
"Heard that one too."

It soon became painfully clear, at least for the moment,
that no amount of cheering could lift Mr. Grumps
out of his sorry, sorry holiday blahs.
"We'll just do all that we can to let Mr. Grumps
know, no matter what, that we do care about him —
and love him," said Mrs. Primm.

One day, a terribly distraught Mr. Grumps
appeared at the Primms' door.
"Loretta! Loretta! Oh, my poor, sweet, Loretta!" he cried.
"What's happened to Loretta!" Mrs. Primm exclaimed.
"She's gone; vanished; slipped out as I signed for a package.
Loretta is lost!" Mr. Grumps wept.

"Oh, no!" everyone cried out.
Loretta lost! Lyle was thunderstruck.
"Loretta! Loretta!" Mr. Grumps sobbed away.

Immediately, the family spread out
in search of Loretta.
Mrs. Primm circled the neighborhood
in her car.

Joshua and Miranda
questioned people on
the street.

Mr. Primm and Lyle
looked everywhere,
late into the night.
No Loretta.

No one slept that night.
Lyle kept a constant vigil at the window,
anxiously searching the street below
for signs of Loretta. Chilling visions of Loretta
wandering alone or caught up in all manner
of dangerous scrapes haunted him.

Suddenly Lyle knew all too clearly what he
wanted most for Christmas — but much sooner, please.
"I want the safe return of Loretta," he whispered to himself.

117

The next day, the family was
posting notices everywhere about Loretta
and handing out flyers.

Mr. Grumps offered a handsome reward,
and many strays were brought to his door.
"No, that's not Loretta. Sorry, not that one either.
Nor that one," he said, sadly turning one after
another away. "But do, please, try to find good homes
for these cats," he always urged them.

At long last, Mr. Grumps
had something meaningful
to be unhappy about.
"Where, oh where, is she?"
he cried out again and again.

So where indeed was Loretta?
Well, after spending a shivery, terrifying night
far away from East 88th Street,
she was, at this exact moment, having
serious second thoughts about running away.

True, she had had her fill of grumpy Mr. Grumps,
but now she began to miss him — miss him desperately,
blahs and all. And she missed her friends; but mostly Lyle.

The world away from home was a lonely place,
she sadly decided — especially at Christmas.

"Ah, what have we here?"
Loretta soon found herself
staring up at the grinning face
of Prunella Kitt,
known in the neighborhood
as the Cat Lady.

"And oh, so pretty," Prunella chortled.
"All alone, are you? No home?
No one to look after you — to feed you?
Oh, you poor, shriveled darling. Well, not to worry.
Prunella is here. And Prunella will take good care of you."

Prunella scooped Loretta up, put her in a basket,
and scurried home.

With quick steps Prunella climbed the rickety stairs
to her third floor rooms.

At the landing she met an upstairs neighbor.
And that neighbor was none other than
Hector P. Valenti, Star of Stage and Screen.
"Lookie-look, will you," said Prunella, proudly lifting
the lid of her basket.
"Not another cat, Prunella!" Hector rolled his eyes.
"Yes, and isn't she a precious little lambkin!"
Prunella cooed in a baby voice.

"Adorable." Hector shook his head in disbelief
as he rushed off to work.

Prunella entered her apartment and
immediately set Loretta free.
"Welcome home, my darling," she said.
Loretta blinked with amazement.
It was instantly clear that Prunella never met a cat
she didn't like. Her place swarmed with cats —
cats here, cats there;
cats, cats, cats, galore, everywhere.

And some weren't at all nice.
Now, more than ever, Loretta longed
to be home.

Meanwhile, the search for Loretta went on.
Posting still another notice, Lyle and Mrs. Primm
suddenly heard a familiar voice call to them from inside
a house. They soon discovered the voice belonged to
Lyle's former dance partner, Hector P. Valenti,
Star of Stage and Screen.

The old friends were delighted to see each other.
But what was Hector up to now?
Well, at the moment it seemed he was very busy
cleaning windows.
"Oh, do you live here?" asked Mrs. Primm.

Hector came to the door.
"Actually, I work here," he answered.
"I perform star-quality house-cleaning services.
It's an interesting little side venture — ahem,
between stage and screen engagements, of course."
"Yes, of course," said Mrs. Primm.

Lyle immediately gave Hector a flyer about Loretta.
Hector read it with great interest — especially the part
about the reward. He looked carefully at Loretta's picture.
Suddenly bells went off in his head.
"I can find Loretta," he announced.

Lyle and Mrs. Primm were overjoyed.
"Oh, please, let's get her at once," said Mrs. Primm.
"Not so fast," said Hector. "The people I work for
will want a clean house when they return."
"Oh, but we must find Loretta!" Mrs. Primm pleaded.

Hector had an idea. "Come in, please," he said.
Hector took off his apron and put it on Lyle.
"I'm sure you'll know what to do, Lyle," said Hector.

"I don't think Lyle should be doing this,"
said Mrs. Primm. But Lyle's cheerful smile
encouraged Mrs. Primm to leave with Hector.

"Good-bye, dear," said Mrs. Primm. "We won't
be long, I'm sure."
"See you later," said Hector. "And do, please,
remember to dust under the beds."

Lyle was so delighted at the prospect of finding Loretta,
he got to work at once — and with great enthusiasm.
He scrubbed the dishes thoroughly in hot sudsy water . . .

and admired
his reflection
in their gleaming
brightness.

After polishing the silverware, Lyle went on
to make the beds. As always, he was proud of
his hospital corners and pictured how pleased
the homeowners would be when they returned.

After that there was the usual scrubbing,
dusting, sweeping, and waxing.

To lighten his house cleaning chores,
Lyle decided to have fun with floor waxing
by pretending to do a television commercial.

"See my shiny waxed floor," he made believe he was saying.
"Isn't it beautiful? Isn't it gorgeous? Want to know my secret?
Dazzle. That's right folks, Dazzle Floor Wax. So if you want your
floor to sparkle like mine, rush out this very instant, if not sooner,
and get yourself some Dazzle. And do get the giant economy size.
Take it from Lyle, you won't be sorry. Oh, and by the way, friends,
remember our slogan: Dazzle Dazzles."

Lyle was so pleased
with his commercial,
he began to dance.

OOPS! The waxed floor was slippery, and he fell —
kerplunk! — at the feet of Mr. and Mrs. Worthmore,
the owners of the house, who had just come home.
They were not amused.

In fact, they were so astonished to find
a crocodile prancing about the house, Mrs. Worthmore
promptly fainted as Mr. Worthmore managed,
somehow, to call the police.

The police arrived and arrested Lyle.
He was charged with breaking in.
News of his arrest was broadcast
far and wide.

Later, in court, the judge was about to have
Lyle locked up when Mrs. Primm, Hector,
and Prunella burst in — with Loretta.
Lyle's eyes lit up the instant he saw Loretta.

"Please, your honor," Mrs. Primm pleaded,
"Lyle is innocent. He was merely helping to clean
so Hector could be free to find Loretta."
"Is this true?" asked the judge.
"Yes, your honor," said Hector.
"And where exactly was Loretta?" asked the judge.
"Safe and sound in my home," Prunella spoke up proudly.

When they heard this, Mr. and Mrs. Worthmore,
who were also in court, immediately dropped the charges.
They even commended Lyle for doing an outstanding job
cleaning their house.
"Best we ever had," said Mrs. Worthmore,
looking scornfully at Hector.
"Case dismissed," said the judge.

On Christmas Eve, Mr. Grumps gave a dinner party.
Everyone was invited: the Primms, Lyle and his mother,
Hector, Prunella, and even Mr. and Mrs. Worthmore.
Besides sharing the reward for finding Loretta,
Hector and Prunella seemed, also, to share a blossoming
fondness for one another.
"We will need to find good homes for your cats, Prunella,"
said Hector. "We'll be on the road so much, you know."
"Oh, of course, Hector, dear," Prunella said, adoringly.

Mr. Grumps and Loretta were blissfully reunited.
"Friends, this is a most joyous, meaningful night,"
said Mr. Grumps, "and so, I say to one and all,
merry, merry Christmas —
and good-bye forever to the blahs."
Everyone smiled . . .

especially Lyle and Loretta.

WE THREE KINGS

WE THREE KINGS of Orient are;
Bearing gifts we traverse afar,
Field and fountain, moor and mountain,
Following yonder star.

Star of wonder, star of night,
Star of royal beauty bright,
Westward leading, still proceeding,
Guide us to the perfect light.

Born a King on Bethlehem's plain.
Gold I bring to crown Him again.
King forever, ceasing never,
Over us all to reign.

Glorious now, behold Him arise,
King and God and Sacrifice.
Alleluia, alleluia,
Earth to the heav'ns replies.

For John — who waited . . .
and waited for this book

Merry Christmas, Ollie!

Olivier Dunrea

This is Gossie.
This is Gertie.
They are waiting.

This is BooBoo.
This is Peedie.
They are waiting.

This is Ollie.

He is waiting.

The goslings are waiting.
Waiting for Christmas.
Waiting for Father Christmas
Goose!

Gossie and Gertie peek
over the wall.

They hang their bright-colored
boots in the barn.

BooBoo and Peedie peer
around the beehive.

They hang their striped
stockings in the barn.

Ollie stomps through the snow.

"I want Christmas!" he shouts.

Ollie stomps to Gossie and Gertie.

"Is Christmas here yet?" he asks.

"Christmas is coming,"
Gossie whispers.
"Father Christmas Goose is
coming," Gertie whispers.

Ollie stomps to BooBoo and Peedie.

"Is Christmas here yet?" he asks.

"Christmas is almost here,"
Peedie whispers.
"Father Christmas Goose
will bring lots of food,"
BooBoo whispers.

"I want Christmas NOW!"
shouts Ollie.

"Listen!" shout Gossie
and Gertie.

"He's coming!" shout BooBoo
and Peedie.

Four small goslings scurry
to their nests.

One small gosling hops
through the snow.

Ollie listens.
Ollie looks.

Ollie waits.
And waits.

Snow falls. Bells jingle.
"Merry Christmas, Ollie!"

"Christmas is here!" shouts Ollie.

DECK THE HALL

DECK THE HALL with boughs of holly.
Fa-la-la-la-la, la-la-la-la.
'Tis the season to be jolly.
Fa-la-la-la-la, la-la-la-la.
Don we now our gay apparel.
Fa-la-la-la-la-la, la-la-la.
Troll the ancient Yuletide carol.
Fa-la-la-la-la, la-la-la-la.
See the blazing Yule before us.
Fa-la-la-la-la, la-la-la-la.
Strike the harp and join the chorus.
Fa-la-la-la-la, la-la-la-la.

Follow me in merry measure
Fa-la-la-la-la-la, la-la-la.
While I tell of Yuletide treasure.
Fa-la-la-la-la, la-la-la-la.
Fast away the old year passes.
Fa-la-la-la-la, la-la-la-la.
Hail the new, ye lads and lasses.
Fa-la-la-la-la, la-la-la-la.
Sing we joyous, all together,
Fa-la-la-la-la-la, la-la-la.
Heedless of the wind and weather.
Fa-la-la-la-la, la-la-la-la.

To Judy, with love

A Small Christmas

by Wong Herbert Yee

In the middle of town, where buildings stand tall,

There lives a little man called Fireman Small.

The only fireman this side of the bay

Is getting ready for the holiday!

Since no calls have come in, he's also free

To help Mayor Mole find a Christmas tree.

On Beaver's Tree Farm, they grow pines big and tall
And some *teeny-tiny*, like Fireman Small.
With a few mighty WHACKS! he chops a tree down,
Throws it on the truck, and drives back to town.

The city is bustling with yuletide cheer.

For stores it's the busiest time of the year.

Fireman Small waves to a holiday shopper

As he straightens the Christmas tree topper.

There are bundles of lights that need to get strung,

Boxes of ornaments waiting to be hung.

The townsfolk hustle past Small on the street.

Some stop to sample a warm winter treat.

Boys and girls climb onto Santa's lap.

Moms and dads line up with presents to wrap.

Soon it's time for shopkeepers to leave,
Since stores all close early on Christmas Eve.
Fireman Small puts up the last decoration.
Tired and beat, he drives back to the station.

He pulls the truck into firehouse nine,

Walks upstairs one step at a time.

Closes the curtains, gets in bed,

And pulls the covers over his head.

Around midnight, he hears a sound on the roof,
A jingling of sleigh bells, the *tip-tap* of hoof.
There's a CRASH! . . . then a muffled *ho-ho-ho*.
Someone's downstairs in the firehouse below!

Quickly out of bed he scoots,
Jumps into his pants and boots.
Ready to go, he slides down the pole,
Sees two legs sticking out of the coal!

Black boots, a brown sack, white bearded jaws . . .

Is it a burglar? Why—it's Santa Claus!

From the cap on his head right down to each foot,

The jolly old fellow is covered in soot!

His clothes get tossed in the washing machine.

In just a short while, they're dry and clean!

Uh-oh! Something's wrong. The red suit has *shrunk!*

Worse than that, Santa's asleep in his bunk!

What about all the good girls and boys?

Who will deliver the rest of the toys?

Though Fireman Small should be snuggled in bed,

He races up to the rooftop instead.

Dressed in Santa's suit, he hops in the sleigh.

But the reindeer refuse to fly away!

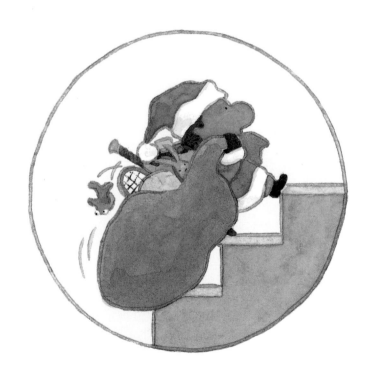

What can he do now? Such *terrible* luck!

Wait! Fireman Small can take the fire truck!

Out of the station, he's ready to go,

Plowing through streets all covered with snow.

Fireman Small clutches the sack full of toys.

He slides down the chimney without any noise.

At Farmer Pig's farm, he leaves a straw hat,
New overalls, and a chew toy for Cat.
Beaver's gift is her own Ping-Pong paddle.
Rabbit gets a rocking horse and a saddle.

Up the chimney he scoots in a hurry.

Down the rooftop he shoots with a flurry.

Fireman Small speeds along to the next house,
Dropping off presents for Possum and Mouse.

He stuffs a stocking for Crocodile's daughter.

Makes sure the Christmas tree has enough water.

Fireman Small crosses each name off his list.

The bag is empty. No one has been missed.

He pulls back into station number nine.

Walks upstairs, one step at a time.

Stretches and yawns, crawls into bed . . .

And pulls the covers over his head.

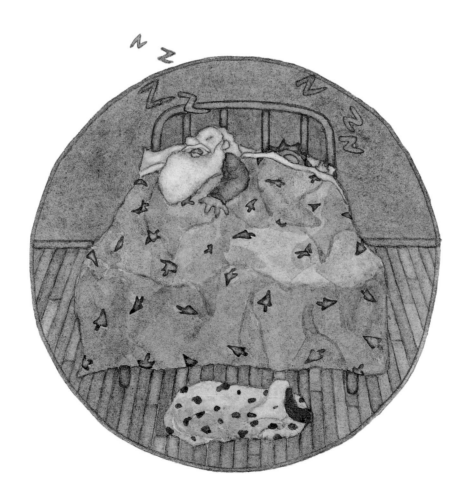

When Fireman Small gets up on Christmas Day,

He finds no Santa, no reindeer or sleigh.

Was it a dream? Did he imagine it all?

Look! There's a letter for Fireman Small:

After flying all night,
North, south, east, and west,
My reindeer and I
Were in need of some rest.
Thank you, Fireman Small,
You're a fine substitute.
Please keep this token,
My now tiny red suit!

LITTLE TOWN OF BETHLEHEM

O LITTLE TOWN of Bethlehem,
How still we see thee lie.
Above thy deep and dreamless sleep
The silent stars go by.
Yet in thy dark streets shineth
The everlasting light.
The hopes and fears of all the years
Are met in thee tonight.

For Christ is born of Mary,
And gathered all above,
While mortals sleep, the angels keep
Their watch of wond'ring love.
O morning stars, together
Proclaim the Holy birth!
And praises sing to God the King,
And peace to all on earth.

Merry Christmas, Strega Nona

STORY AND PICTURES BY

TOMIE de PAOLA

♥ for Maria,
my editor and friend.

It was the first Sunday of Advent,
and everyone in the little town in Calabria
was busy getting ready for Christmas.

Including Strega Nona — Grandma Witch.
She was busy getting everything ready
for the Christmas Eve feast
that she prepared every year.

Big Anthony, who worked for Strega Nona,
was being kept busy, too!

"Anthony," said Strega Nona, "don't dawdle!
There are only four weeks to *Natale* — Christmas —
and there is so much to do.
"The whole house must be cleaned,
and there is so much cooking and baking to do.
After all, everybody in the town will be here."

"Why can't Bambolona help?" whined Big Anthony.
Bambolona was the baker's daughter
who had come to stay with Strega Nona
and learn her magic.

"Bambolona has gone to help her father at the bakery,"
answered Strega Nona.

With Christmas coming, the poor baker was in such trouble
with so many people asking for special cakes and cookies
that he didn't even have time to sit in the square
with his friends.
Bambolona and Strega Nona felt sorry for him.
So Strega Nona sent Bambolona home to help.

"Why don't you help the baker out with your magic,
Strega Nona?" asked Big Anthony.
"No, not at Christmas!" said Strega Nona.
"Now, go shake out those feather beds."

"Anthony," said Strega Nona,
"run down the hill to the town and get me a new broom
so we can sweep the house from top to bottom."
"Oh, Strega Nona," said Big Anthony,
"can't we sweep the house with magic?"
"Not at Christmastime," said Strega Nona.
So Big Anthony went down the hill
to get a new broom.

Strega Nona worked hard
cleaning the house from top to bottom
as the days of Advent went by.

Each week she lit one more candle
on the Advent wreath.

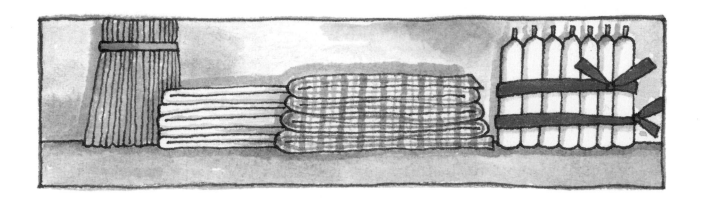

And each day, she sent Big Anthony
on an errand down to the town.
New brooms, new candles, new curtains,
new bedcovers, new tablecloth.
"Anthony," said Strega Nona,
"run down the hill and get me the *baccalà* —
the dried codfish for the Christmas stew.
And when you get back,
put it in the tub with water to soak it."
"Soak it?" asked Big Anthony.

"Yes," answered Strega Nona.
"Every day, until Christmas Eve, you must change the water
so the fish will be nice and soft
and not too salty for the Christmas stew."

"Can't your magic do all that?" asked Big Anthony.
"No, no magic at Christmastime," said Strega Nona.
"Christmas has a magic of its own."
So Big Anthony set off down the hill.

"Hello, Big Anthony," said one of the townspeople.
"How's Strega Nona?"
"Oh," said Big Anthony, "she's very busy
getting the house ready for Christmas.
Every day she sends me to town to get something.
Every day she has me helping her clean windows,
shake out the beds, paint the goat shed.
She's getting ready to cook all kinds of things.
I have to soak the codfish — the *baccalà* —
and change the water every day until Christmas Eve.
And I'm tired!"

"Don't you know
that Strega Nona loves *Natale* — Christmas?" a man from town asked.
"That's why she's so busy!
Why, she doesn't even have time to cure headaches
and make love potions and get rid of warts."
"Every year she cleans her house and prepares
a big feast and invites everyone," said a woman.
"She invites everyone?" asked Big Anthony.
"Everyone," said the woman. "Why, it wouldn't
seem *Natale* without the feast at Strega Nona's house."

"Hello, Big Anthony," said Bambolona,
who was on her way to the bakery.
"Are you in town
to buy Strega Nona a Christmas gift?"

"Oh, Bambolona,
I want to talk with you about that,"
said Big Anthony.

One by one the days went by,
and finally it was the day of Christmas Eve —
la Vigilia di Natale.

"Now, Anthony," said Strega Nona,
"here is a long list of things
for you to get for me — flour, eggs, butter, spices,
peppers, olives, oil, and sugar.
Hurry down the hill and hurry right home again,
for I have all kinds of things
to cook and bake."
"Oh, Strega Nona," Big Anthony complained,
"can't you use —?"
"NO MAGIC AT CHRISTMASTIME," said Strega Nona.
"Now go! I have to decorate the house
with the lemon blossoms and periwinkles."

Strega Nona waited and waited and waited.
No Big Anthony.
Finally the sun began to set,
and Big Anthony came whistling up the hill —
with empty hands.

"Anthony," said Strega Nona,
standing in the doorway of her little house,
"where have you been?"
"Oh, Strega Nona,
there was a Christmas puppet show in the town square.
It came all the way from Venice, up north."

"And where are all the things on my list?"
"Oh," said Big Anthony, "I forgot."

"Anthony, what am I going to do?
It's Christmas Eve.
There will be no cookies,
no *cenci* — fried pastry — no roasted peppers.
Oh, well, go get me the *baccalà*,
so I can at least make the fish stew."

Big Anthony came back
holding the codfish. It was as stiff as a board.
"I forgot this, too," said Big Anthony.
"I forgot to soak it in the water."
"Oh, Big Anthony, won't you *ever* learn!"
cried Strega Nona.

"Now it's too late to prepare anything
to eat for the feast."
"There's always your magic pasta pot,"
said Big Anthony timidly.
"No! I've told you before — NO MAGIC at Christmas,"
said Strega Nona.
"There will be no Christmas feast
at Strega Nona's this year!"

Strega Nona sent Big Anthony
to tell everyone not to come to her house for the feast.

She looked at the lemon blossoms and periwinkles decorating the house.

Outside, she heard the *Zampognari,*
the shepherds from Abruzzi
who came all the way down to Calabria
to sing Christmas songs.

The bells rang.
It was time for the Midnight Mass.

Sadly,
Strega Nona went down the hill
to the church.
A fine Christmas this would be
with no company, no feast.

The townspeople whispered
as she went into the church.
"No feast," said one.
"Poor us," said another.
POOR Strega Nona.

When the mass was ended,
Strega Nona went up to the big manger scene
in the church.
There beside the Virgin and Saint Joseph
lay the Holy Child.

"Ah, *Bambino*," said Strega Nona,
"the night you were born
it was not like this manger scene,
with all these people.
You were all alone with your mama and Saint Joseph —
all alone, just like Strega Nona is tonight.
Ah — anyway — happy birthday *Bambino,*
and *Buon Natale.*"

And Strega Nona slowly left the dark church

and climbed the hill to her little house.

She opened the door —
and the room burst into light.
"*Buon Natale* — Merry Christmas, Strega Nona!"
everyone cried.
"This year, we're giving *you* a feast."
"Look," said Bambolona,
"codfish stew, roasted peppers,
cookies, and fried pastry."

"Oh, Bambolona," said Strega Nona,
"did you do all this for Strega Nona?"
"No, Strega Nona," said Bambolona.
"Big Anthony planned the whole surprise!"

"Bravo, Big Anthony!" everyone shouted.

"Merry Christmas, Strega Nona," said Big Anthony.
"Oh, Anthony," said Strega Nona.
"You *have* learned! And with NO MAGIC."

"It's just like you said, Strega Nona."
Big Anthony smiled.
"Christmas has a magic of its own."

THE FIRST NOEL

THE FIRST NOEL the angel did say
Was to certain poor shepherds in fields as they lay.
In fields as they lay keeping their sheep
On a cold winter's night that was so deep.

Noel, Noel, Noel, Noel,
Born is the King of Israel.

They looked up and saw a star
Shining in the east, beyond them far.
And to the earth it gave great light,
And so it continued both day and night.

This star drew nigh to the northwest.
And over Bethlehem it took its rest.
And there it did both stop and stay,
Right over the place where Jesus lay.

'Twas the Night Before Christmas

A Visit from St. Nicholas

By Clement C. Moore

With Pictures by Jessie Willcox Smith

'T WAS the night before Christmas, when all through

the house

Not a creature was stirring, not even a mouse;

The stockings were hung by the chimney with care

In hopes that St. Nicholas soon would be there;

HE children were nestled all snug in their beds,

While visions of sugar-plums danced in their heads;

And mamma in her kerchief, and I in my cap,

Had just settled our brains for a long winter's nap,

HEN out on the lawn there arose such a clatter,

I sprang from the bed to see what was the matter.

Away to the window I flew like a flash,

Tore open the shutters and threw up the sash.

HE moon on the breast of the new-fallen snow

Gave the lustre of mid-day to objects below,

When, what to my wondering eyes should appear,

But a miniature sleigh, and eight tiny reindeer,

WITH a little old driver, so lively and quick,

I knew in a moment it must be St. Nick.

More rapid than eagles his coursers they came,

And he whistled, and shouted, and called them by name:

N OW, *Dasher!* now, *Dancer!* now, *Prancer* and *Vixen!*

On, *Comet!* on, *Cupid!* on, *Donder* and *Blitzen!*

To the top of the porch! to the top of the wall!

Now dash away! dash away! dash away all!''

S dry leaves that before the wild hurricane fly,

When they meet with an obstacle, mount to the sky;

So up to the house-top the coursers they flew,

With the sleigh full of Toys, and St. Nicholas too.

A ND then, in a twinkling, I heard on the roof

The prancing and pawing of each little hoof.

As I drew in my head, and was turning around,

Down the chimney St. Nicholas came with a bound.

E was dressed all in fur, from his head to his foot,

And his clothes were all tarnished with ashes and soot;

A bundle of Toys he had flung on his back,

And he looked like a pedler just opening his pack.

IS eyes — how they twinkled! his dimples how merry!

His cheeks were like roses, his nose like a cherry!

His droll little mouth was drawn up like a bow,

And the beard of his chin was as white as the snow;

HE stump of a pipe he held tight in his teeth,

And the smoke it encircled his head like a wreath;

He had a broad face and a little round belly,

That shook when he laughed, like a bowlful of jelly.

E was chubby and plump, a right jolly old elf,

And I laughed when I saw him, in spite of myself;

A wink of his eye and a twist of his head,

Soon gave me to know I had nothing to dread;

E spoke not a word, but went straight to his work,

And filled all the stockings; then turned with a jerk,

And laying his finger aside of his nose,

And giving a nod, up the chimney he rose;

E sprang to his sleigh, to his team gave a whistle,

And away they all flew like the down of a thistle.

But I heard him exclaim, ere he drove out of sight,

"Happy Christmas to all, and to all a good-night."

SILENT NIGHT

SILENT NIGHT, holy night.
All is calm, all is bright.
Round yon Virgin Mother and Child,
Holy Infant so tender and mild.
Sleep in heavenly peace,
Sleep in heavenly peace.

Silent night, holy night.
Shepherds quake at the sight.
Glories stream from heaven afar.
Heav'nly hosts sing Alleluia.
Christ the Savior is born!
Christ the Savior is born.

Silent night, holy night.
Son of God, love's pure light.
Radiant beams from Thy holy face,
With the dawn of redeeming grace.
Jesus, Lord, at Thy birth,
Jesus, Lord, at Thy birth.

Meet the Authors and Illustrators

H. A. AND MARGRET REY

HANS AUGUSTO REY and MARGRET REY escaped Nazi-occupied Paris in 1940 by bicycle, carrying the manuscript for the first book about Curious George. They came to live in the United States, and *Curious George* was published in 1941. You can learn more about the Reys and Curious George and find games, activities, downloads, and PBS television shows at www.curiousgeorge.com.

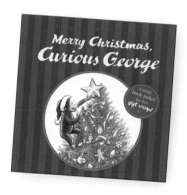 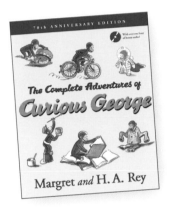  

HELEN LESTER AND LYNN MUNSINGER

HELEN LESTER is a full-time writer who makes her home in Pawling, New York. She has written numerous books featuring everyone's favorite penguin, Tacky, and lots of other memorable characters, often with the illustrator Lynn Munsinger. Visit Helen at www.helenlester.com.

LYNN MUNSINGER is a full-time illustrator who created the Tacky the Penguin series with Helen Lester. They have made more than twenty-five fantastic books together, including *A Porcupine Named Fluffy* and *Hooway for Wodney Wat*. Munsinger divides her time between Connecticut and Vermont.

  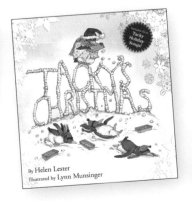 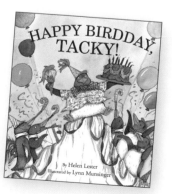

JOHN AND ANN HASSETT

JOHN and ANN HASSETT live in an old yellow farmhouse on the Maine coast with chickens and a dog, and mice in the walls. They've been collaborating on picture books for more than ten years. Their books are known for their quirky humor and lively illustrations. Visit the Hassetts online at www.hassettbooks.com.

BERNARD WABER

BERNARD WABER is the beloved, best-selling author and illustrator of eight books about everyone's favorite crocodile, Lyle. He lives in Baldwin Harbor, New York.

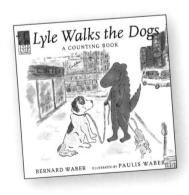

284

OLIVIER DUNREA

OLIVIER DUNREA is the award-winning creator of the best-selling Gossie & Friends books and the author and illustrator of more than fifty children's books. He lives, writes, and paints in a tiny, remote village in the Catskills Mountains in upstate New York. Visit his website at www.olivierdunrea.com.

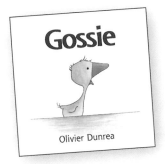
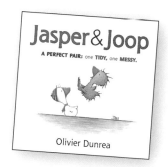

WONG HERBERT YEE

WONG HERBERT YEE lives in Michigan, where he writes and illustrates books for children, including the Mouse and Mole series and the Fireman Small series. For more information, visit his blog at wongherbertyee.blogspot.com.

TOMIE dePAOLA

TOMIE dePAOLA has been published for more than forty years and has written and/or illustrated nearly 250 books, including *Strega Nona, 26 Fairmount Avenue, The Art Lesson,* and *Christmas Remembered.* More than fifteen million copies of his books have sold worldwide. Tomie lives in New London, New Hampshire, with his Airedale terrier, Brontë, and works in a renovated two-hundred-year-old barn. Visit him online at www.tomie.com.

CLEMENT C. MOORE AND JESSIE WILLCOX SMITH

CLEMENT CLARKE MOORE was a writer and professor and is credited with writing "A Visit from St. Nicholas" for his children. Originally published anonymously on December 23, 1823, that poem would come to be known as the famous holiday classic "'Twas the Night Before Christmas."

JESSIE WILLCOX SMITH was a prolific illustrator of magazines and children's books. She was a frequent contributor to *Ladies Home Journal.* Some of her best-known work for children includes Charles Kingsley's *The Water Babies.*

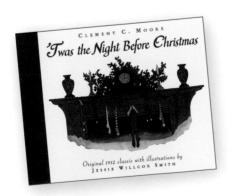

Don't miss these other treasuries filled with special stories for your family to share:

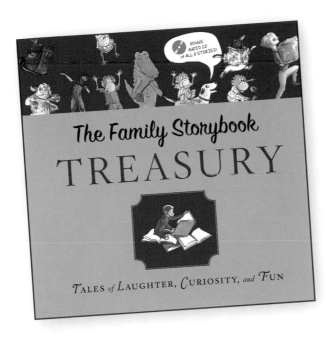

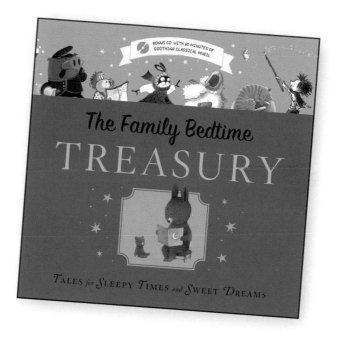